FOR MUM AND DAD
—T. F. & E. F.

The Night Gardener

Terry Fan & Eric Fan

Frances Lincoln
Children's Books

William looked out of his window
to find a commotion on the street.
He quickly dressed, ran downstairs
and raced out of the door to discover…

a wise owl had appeared overnight, as if by magic.
William spent the whole day staring at it in wonder,

and he continued to stare until it
became too dark to see.

That night he went to sleep
with a sense of excitement.

The following morning,

William was not disappointed.

Each day William discovered a new topiary.
Next was a friendly rabbit,

followed by a pretty parakeet…

and then a playful elephant.

With each new sculpture, the crowds grew and grew.

Something was happening on Grimloch Lane.

Something good.

The next day, William dashed out of his home

and followed the crowds, only to find…

the most magnificent masterpiece yet!

Festivities continued
long after the sun had set.

As William was about
to head home,

he spotted someone unfamiliar.

Could it be?

The gentleman turned to William.
"There are so many trees in this park.
I could use a little help."
It *was* the Night Gardener!

Under the light of
a full moon,

they worked deep
into the night.

William awoke to the sound of happy families walking by,

and a gift from the Night Gardener.

The whole town had come out to admire the
Night Gardener's – and William's – hard work.

Over time the leaves changed…

and then fell,

until there was no evidence
that the Night Gardener
had ever been to
Grimloch Lane.

But the people of the small town
were never the same.

And neither was William.